FUNNY

Teasing Tongue-Twisters

DEAD FUNNY

picked by John Foster

Illustrated by Nathan Reed

Collins

An imprint of HarperCollinsPublishers

First published by Collins in 2002
Collins is an imprint of HarperCollins*Publishers* Ltd,
77-85 Fulham Palace Road, Hammersmith, W6 8JB

The HarperCollins website address is:
www.fireandwater.com

1 3 5 7 9 8 6 4 2

This collection copyright © John Foster 2002
Illustrations by Nathan Reed 2002
Back cover poem *Susan Steps Down* copyright © Carol Carman 2002
The acknowledgements on page 96 constitute
an extension of this copyright page.

0 00 711213 0

The authors, illustrator and compiler assert the moral right to
be identified as the authors, illustrator and compiler of this work.

Printed and bound in Great Britain by
Omnia Books Limited
Glasgow

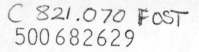

Ruth Lies Still
(an epitaph)

Under this stone, here lies Ruth.

She never, ever told the truth.

She says she's dead, but is this proof?

Are you lying still now, Ruth?

Jane Clarke

Epitaph to a Demon Headmaster
(recently deceased in a mysterious explosion)

We'll miss you, Sir,

no doubt of that.

We wish you all the best.

We hope you find

a pleasant bed of flames

on which to rest.

We'd like to say

we'd visit

but it wouldn't be the truth.

Ascending

would be fine, Sir,

but descending's so uncouth.

Patricia Leighton

Careless Conclusions

"ouch!"

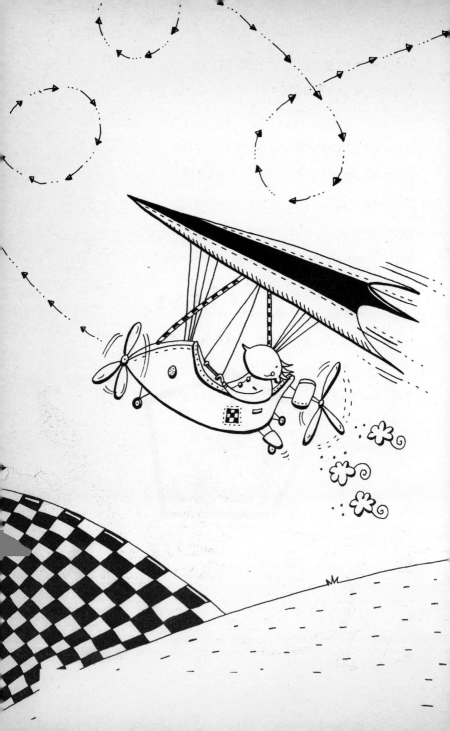

Unhappy Landing
(an epitaph)

Here lie the bones of Wilbur Flytte

Who stole his father's micro-light.

At take-off he was quite an ace

Performing stunts with style and grace.

But, something he had never planned,

No-one taught him how to land.

So, round and round poor Wilbur went,

Till all his precious fuel was spent.

Returning to earth was easy, he found,

But, he landed six feet underground.

David Whitehead

whoops!

Tommy Twigg

Beneath this stone lies Tommy Twigg
Who from a bottle took a swig
He should have checked the bottle first
Before he sought to quench his thirst
For Tommy, lying in this soil
Has overdosed on caster oil!

Brenda Williams

Poor Little Johnny

Poor little Johnny
We'll never see him more –
For what he thought was H_2O
Was H_2SO_4

Anon

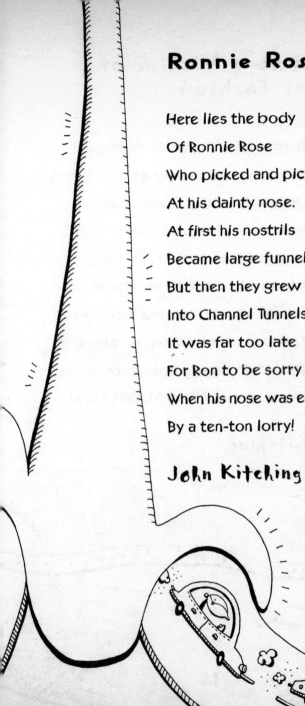

Ronnie Rose

Here lies the body
Of Ronnie Rose
Who picked and picked
At his dainty nose.

At first his nostrils
Became large funnels.
But then they grew
Into Channel Tunnels.

It was far too late
For Ron to be sorry
When his nose was entered
By a ten-ton lorry!

John Kitching

Epitaph to a Victim of Designer Fashion

A warning, in memory of Annabel Hayling,

Whose designer laces were designed to be trailing.

When tied in a bow, as young Annabel said,

The expensive wording just couldn't be read.

Her parents pleaded that Annabel tie them,

But Annabel, foolishly, chose to defy them.

To all who, like her, might disregard warnings

In favour of fashion on dark winter mornings,

Beware of steep stairways and designer crazes,

Remember poor Annabel. DO UP YOUR LACES!

Daphne Kitching

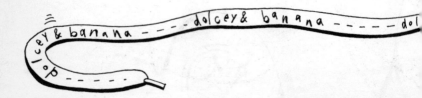

Jumping to a Conclusion

There was an old man who averred
He had learned how to fly like a bird;
Cheered by thousands of people
He leapt from the steeple —
This tomb states the date it occurred.

Anon

Jamie Jack

Here lies the body of Jamie Jack
Who played the fool on a railway track.

Brenda Williams

Susan Steps Down

Susan avoided the cracks with care
And always trod upon the square;
An unwise move, she was to discover –
She stepped on a manhole without a cover.

Carol Carman

Jane

Jane read the notice with great care:

'Man-Eating Tiger – Please Beware.'

And though she could see that the tiger was wild,

She didn't think it would eat a small child.

For the notice implied that, though it ate men,

It never ate women or little children.

In thinking this, she was misled.

And, consequently, Jane is dead.

Cynthia Rider

16

Dutch Courage

Jan loved
Round the windmill jogs
Tripped and fell –
Popped his clogs.

Ruth Underhill

Anna

Here lies the body of our Anna
Done to death by a banana.
It wasn't the fruit that laid her low
But the skin of the thing that made her go.

Anon

Arlene

Beneath this sombre yew tree lie
The ashes of Arlene,
Who tried to light the barbecue
With a can of gasoline.

Barbara Moore

Monstrous
Memorials

Epitaph for Frankenstein

When Frankenstein's Monster finally died,
And his reign of terror ceased,
These were the words they inscribed on his grave:
'May the occupant Rust in Peace.'

Clive Webster

Judgement Day

He will not be back
He will not see you later
This robot is no more
Now an Ex-Terminator.

Paul Cookson

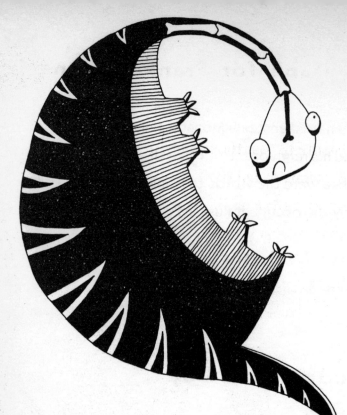

Two Dinosaur Epitaphs

Alive and well no longer

The mighty Brontosaurus

Exit to extinction

The dead-and-gone-to-saurus.

No more to roar those monstrous jaws

Nor talons or tail flex

Goodbye the king of dinosaurs

Tyrannosaurus – Ex.

Paul Cookson

R.I.P.

Count Zoffin
1836-?

Here rests the body
Of vampire 'Count Zoffin'
Who isn't yet dead
Just asleep in his coffin.

'Fangs for the memories'

Richard Caley

Grave Anagram

R.I.P.

V. EAM

HEADSTONED

1881

'Maybe a garlic covered stake

will make sure that he doesn't wake!'

[Answer – VAMPIRE – HE'S NOT DEAD]

Liz Brownlee

Dracula

Here lies Dracula
He's either on his backula
Or standing right behind you
Getting ready to attackula.

Kaye Umansky

Nursery Epitaphs

Here lies the body
 Of Contrary Mary,
Poisoned by milk
From the local dairy.

Here lies the body
Of Cinderella
Stabbed to death
By her sister's umbrella.

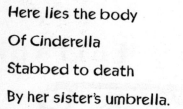

Here lies the body
Of Little Boy Blue —
Swallowed his horn
And it slid right through.

Here lies the body
Of Little Boy Peep
Trampled to death
By a very large sheep.

Here lies the body
Of Little Miss Muffet
Bitten by a spider
Hiding in her tuffet.

Here lies the body
Of Little Jack Horner
Ate too much Christmas pie
And dropped dead in his corner.

Here lies the body
Of Winnie the Pooh.
He poohed too much
And died in a zoo.

Here lies the body
Of Mr Toad
Squashed by a lorry
On a very busy road.

John Kitching

Grave Consequences

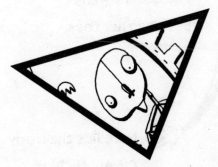

Here lies the body
Of Tony Welch:
Exploded
With a mighty belch.

Here lies the body
Of Mary Rose
She ate the gunge
Between her toes.

Here lies the body
Of Auntie Betty:
Jogged thirty miles
Drowned – far too sweaty.

Here lies the body
Of Bernard Bales:
Died choking
On his well-chewed nails.

Here lies the body
Of Tracey Plumb:
Sucked her body away –
– Began with her thumb!

Here lies the body
Of young Len Loader,
Gassed to death
By his body odour.

John Kitching

Some Grave Consequences of School Trips to Castles

In the dismal gloom
Of a haunted room
Stood a sweet little girl called Beth.
A hundred skeletons
Rattled their bones,
And a headless phantom
Moaned and groaned,
And Beth was scared to death!

'Teacher, Teacher, Freddie Oates
Is trying to swim across the moat.'
Teacher said with a knowing smile,
'That's where the Duke keeps a crocodile.
Let's hope that Freddie's a very good swimmer
Or else he'll spoil the crocodile's dinner.'

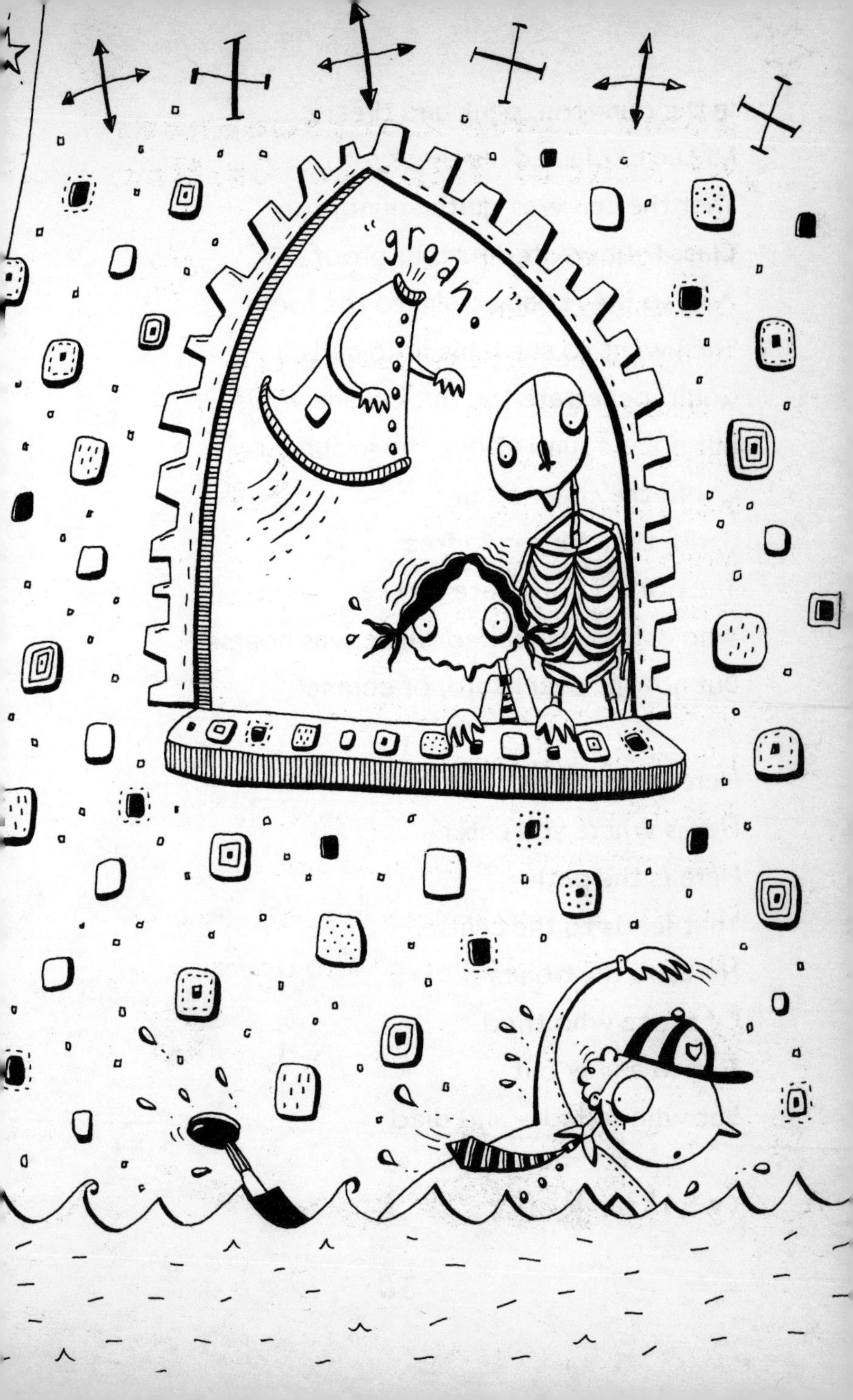
"groan!"

In the dungeon, dank and dreary,

Mr Lee explained his theory

That the cell was quite soundproof.

Class Four wanted further proof

And so they chained him to the roof,

Then went to see if his loud calls

Could penetrate the thick stone walls.

But not a sound above the ground

Could they hear at all.

Sadly, they forgot to free

The poor unfortunate Mr Lee,

Who called and called till he was hoarse,

But no-one ever heard, of course!

Here is the maze.

Here's where you enter.

Here is the path

That leads to the centre.

Here are the bones

Of those who tried

To find a way out

But who failed – and died.

Cynthia Rider

Larry the Liar

Here lies Larry the Liar.
Burnt to death
When his pants caught fire.

Bill Condon

Georgina

Beneath this stone Georgina lies
She ate too many fast food fries
She ate them like she could not stop
Till finally, she just went POP!

Brenda Williams

A Heavy Penalty

Here lies a man who met his fate
Because he put on too much weight.
To over-eating he was prone
But now he's gained his final STONE.

Anon

A Precocious Insomniac Tot

Here lies a precocious, insomniac tot
Who knew how to let down the sides of his cot.
He undid the catches one evening at seven
And, the bars having vanished, fell straight up to
heaven.

Roy Fuller

Really Implausible People

Jim `Houseproud´ Groover

Here lie
The ashes
Of Jim 'Houseproud' Groover
Who sucked himself up
With a powerful Hoover.

Lindsay Macrae

Miss Chit-Chat

Beneath this stone Miss Chit-Chat lies,
Her gossiping days are done,
Her last words were as she passed away:
'I'm just dying to tell someone.'

John Foster

Charlotte Cul-de-sac

In memory of Charlotte Cul-de-sac,
A loyal and trusted friend.
She finally lived up to her name
And came to a dead end.

John Foster

Funny Bones Jones

Here lies Funny Bones Jones,
A lively bloke,
Whose dying groans were,
'What a joke!'

Mary Green

Reginald Hacking

Here lies the body
Of Reginald Hacking.

It was his cough
That bore him off.

John Foster

Death of a Dog Burglar

When he broke in the Rottweiler kennels one night
He wasn't expecting to die
But the teeth in the dark were monstrous and sharp
He should have let sleeping dogs lie.

Paul Cookson

Epitaph to the Late Henry Hackett

Here lie the remains
of one Henry Hackett
minus the arm
they left in his jacket
when getting him ready
for bed in his coffin.
It wasn't a worry –
they said it was nothing
that couldn't be handled,
they'd send it on later
by posthumous post,
to Henry's Creator.

Gina Douthwaite

Hiya, Cynth

'Please mark my grave
with just one flower,'
That was the wish
of Cynthia Tower,
So when she died
they raised a plinth
and marked upon it
'Hiya, Cynth'.

Wes Magee

The Strong Man

He was as proud as a peacock
and brave as a lion, solid as a rock
and as straight as a pine.
He swam like a fish
and ran like a gazelle.

There wasn't a sport
that he didn't do well.
He could soar like a bird
on the flying trapeze.
He could lift mighty weights
and not sag at the knees.
He was daft as a brush though
and went much too far
(although strong as an ox)
when he lifted a car
which was built like a tank.
They found him next day
squashed flat as a pancake
and took him away
dead as a doornail.
His ghost followed on
cool as a cucumber,
winked, and was gone.

Marian Swinger

Annabel Smedley

Here lies

The body

Of Annabel Smedley

Who took an eternity pill

Which proved deadly.

Lindsay Macrae

`Dithering´ Freddy

Here lies

The top half

Of 'Dithering' Freddy

The rest will come soon

When it feels

That it's ready.

Lindsay Macrae

Highway Endings

Highway Endings

Here lies the body
Of Jonathan Bickley;
Tried to cross the road
Too quickly.

Here lies the body
Of Nathan Bell;
Drove just like a bat
From Hell.

Here lies the body
Of Tracey Stead;
Ignored the sign:
'Road works ahead'.

Here lies the body
Of Kevin Turner;
A very, very careless
Learner.

Here lies the body
Of Sammy Sloan
Buried
With his mobile phone.

Here lies the body
Of Anthony Joad;
Aged 93:
Knew his Highway Code.

John Kitching

Epitaph for Elijah

Here lies Elijah

A motor bike rider

He went down a tunnel

Which should have been wider.

Trevor Millum

Mike O'Day

This is the grave of Mike O'Day,
Who died maintaining his right of way,
His right was clear, his will was strong,
But he's just as dead as if he'd been wrong.

Anon

Epitaph for a Know-All

There's nothing Roger didn't know
(Except that red does not mean Go).

J. Patrick Lewis

He Passed the Bobby
Without Any Fuss

He passed the bobby without any fuss,

And he passed the cart of hay,

He tried to pass a swerving bus

And then he passed away.

Anon

Speeding Vicar

He drove too fast. Now the Reverand Jervis
and his car have both had their final service.

Charles Thomson

Traffic Warden

At the traffic warden's grave
no-one stops to pine,
on account of the meter
and double-yellow line!

Andrew Collett

Fast Away

Here lie
The remains
Of 'Fast' Eddy Jakes
Who invented a sports car
Without any brakes.

Lindsay Macrae

Shelby Sharp

Here lie till Gabriel's trumpet peal
The bones of Shelby Sharp.
He dozed while holding a steering wheel
And woke up holding a harp.

Anon

Passed Professionals

The Teacher

Here lies the teacher
who stayed in the warm
while making his pupils
go out in the storm

While they were braving
the snow and the slush
the building collapsed
and the teacher was crushed.

Andrea Shavick

For a Sailor

Long time no sea,
Unfathomably.

For a Gardener

Once he came to plants
With ants.
Now he's come to terms
With worms.

For a Magician

With every trick,
The people cheered!
Except the last...
He disappeared.

For an Electrician

Bad news.
Hot-wired
Short fuse...
Expired.

For a Retired
Australian Traveller

No wander
Down Under.
No wonder
Down under.

For a Beautician

Once her nails had dried,
She curled up 'n' dyed.

J. Patrick Lewis

A Schoolmistress

A schoolmistress called Binks lies here.
She held her own for twenty year.
She pleaded, biffed, said: 'I'm your friend.'
But children got her in the end.

Roy Fuller

Green Fingers

Here lies the body
of a gardener from Leeds,
so do please take a cutting
if you're after some seeds!

Andrew Collett

Stephen Crotchet, Musician

Stephen and time
Are now both even.
Stephen beat time
Now time's beat Stephen.

Anon

Baker

A baker here for ever lies
Fell in an oven and failed to rise.

Peter Bennett

On a Weaver

She was not deft,

With her weft,

Now she winds her warp,

To the sound of a harp.

John Cunliffe

A Sticky End

HERE LIES

glue factory owner, Michael Mend.

Tragically came to a sticky end.

Colin Macfarlane

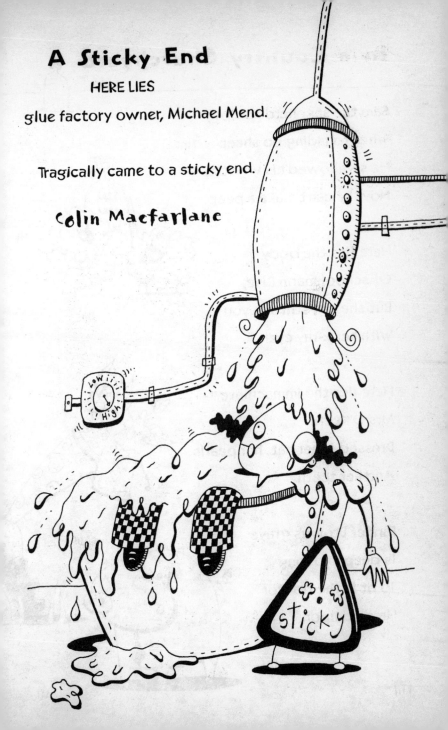

In a Country Churchyard

Sam the shepherd's below,
When rounding up sheep
He swallowed his whistle,
Now he can't make a peep.

Here lies the body
Of school marm Blye,
But she can still see you
With her x-ray eye!

Here lies the immaculate
Mrs O'Keefe
Dressed in her hat, her pearls
And her teeth.

Farmer Brown's grave
Is deep and long
To fit in the tractor
He died upon.

Bob crafted beautiful candles,
He never ever muffed it,
One day he made his best one yet
But then, alas, he snuffed it.

Here lies the wife
Of Archie, the miller,
Some say she did slip,
Some say he did kill 'er.

coral Rumble

Bridging the Cavity

Here lies a dentist
From Haywards Heath,
Consumed by worms
And not by grief;
This hole he fills —
Not clients' teeth.

Trevor Harvey

Dead Money

Sir Donald, now dead,
a debt collector by trade,
gives notice here
that he still wants to be paid.

Andrew Collett

The Escapologist

Here lies an escapologist
Who chose to spend his days
In thinking up ingenious ways
Of breaking open chains and locks
And escaping from a box.

Within a coffin now he lies
For all eternity,
Which seems a cruel twist of fate
For one accustomed to escape.
But if, from here, he rises,
He really will surprise us!

Cynthia Rider

R.I.P.

Here lies a poet
Who was fond of rhyme,
This is the poem he was writing
When he ran out of

Celia Warren

Rosehip the Fortune Teller

Rosehip, the fortune teller,
here lies dead,
she could have saved herself
if she'd only looked ahead.

Andrew Collett

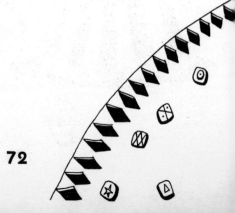

Constable Chest

Here lies the body
Of Constable Chest
His heart made him
He last arrest.

John Foster

Percy Thistle: Football Referee

Here lies the body
Of Percy Thistle,
A ref who's blown
His final whistle.

John Foster

Resting Pets

Resting Pets

Here lies our pet koala bear
Who feared the sound of thunder;
Out went his light in a storm one night
And now he's back down under.

Here lies our mouse, our precious Buck,
Run down one day by a ten-ton truck;
We were fairly certain Buck was dead
When we found his whiskers in the tyre tread.
Buck, oh Buck, what rotten luck,
Foully struck by a ten-ton truck.
To say, 'Here lies' is a cruel myth
There was nothing left to bury you with.

Beneath this stone lie the flesh and bone
Of our cockatoo, Renato;
He died of the blight in the middle of the night
When he swallowed a green tomato.

Here lies a pet camel
So cold in the ground;
You can tell it's his grave
By the big double mound.

Here lies Flossie

Our favourite pussy;

Frequently bossy,

Occasionally fussy;

Her grave is grassy,

Rather than mossy,

Cos mossy's not classy

Enough for Flossie.

Here lies the body of our dog Mac

Who once ran away and never came back.

Stranger, tread softly

Our budgie's gone West;

And somewhere round here

We laid her to rest.

Jack Ousbey

Almost an Epitaph

Missed by a lorry:
Very near squeak;
Cat flu:
At Death's door for a week;
Involved in a fight
With a vicious cur:
Escaped with considerable
Loss of fur;
Nearly poisoned —
Water polluted;
Live wire!
Nearly electrocuted;
Almost drowned
By a seventh wave;
Met a motor mower:
Very close shave!

Fell from a height —
Sixteen floors!
Luckily landed
On all four paws.

Eight lives gone,
Just one to go:
Taking no chances,
Avoiding aggro.

Eric Finney

Our Hamster Patches

Here lie the bones
Of our hamster, Patches,
Who left this earth
Whilst nibbling matches.

He took great delight
In chewing and churning,
Till he chewed the brimstone,
Which left his fur burning.

So lock up your hamsters,
Remember poor Patches,
And if you must light things,
Well, use *safety* matches.

Daphne Kitching

My Thin Friend

Here lies the body
Of stick insect Fred
He didn't move for three whole days
I hope he *was* dead.

Roger Stevens

In Memory of Fido

Here lies Fido, Oh the Grief,
How we will miss his gnashing teeth,
Thief of all our Sunday roasts,
Pray that he's now biting ghosts!

Andrew Fusek Peters

Last Laughs

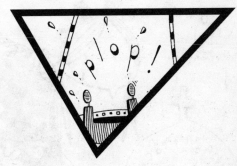

Cut Off

Here lies my dearest friend,
Truer than any other,
Taken tragically young
By my murdering mother,
Who I'll never speak to again
Now that I walk alone.
I lay these daisies on your grave
My beloved Mobile Phone.

PS It would have been lilies only I seem to have run
up this rather huge debt...

Frances Nagle

Slipped Away

Here lies a carrot
And some lumps of coal
The remains of Snowman
Rest his soul

Celia Warren

With Us Always

Here lies Polly Thene.

Her life was very short,

But still her presence lingers

And is never far from thought.

She was used and then discarded,

But now since her release

Remains for all eternity

In an everlasting piece.

Each street, each field, each wood, each stream

Reminds us of our sorrow,

For the body that lies here at rest

Will still be here tomorrow.

Pat Moon

Here Lies...

In life, it's said, even as a youth,
He found it hard to tell the truth.
Meet him, he'd poke you in the ribs,
Laugh — and then start telling fibs.
On mobile phone or walkie-talkie
You'd hear him telling many a porky.
A whopper told, a tall tale spun:
This was his idea of fun.

In death, which now has come to claim him,
He's silent, so why should we blame him?
Of dead men we must not speak ill,
And yet it's true that he lies still.

Eric Finney

Just As Well

We did not care for Henry Holmes
Who kicked defenceless garden gnomes
And if we knew, we would not tell
Who kicked *him* down the wishing well!

Sue Cowling

Lady Godiva

Here lies Lady Godiva
She didn't wear a bra
Or knickers iva.

The Boy on the Burning Deck

The boy stood on the burning deck
Jumped to safety—
Broke his neck.

Roger McGough

Rest in Peace

Here lies lazy Lizzie.

Always idle, never busy.

Rest in peace, I hear you say.

Lizzie does so. Every day.

Ann Bonner

Back to Back

Here lies the body of our friend Jack,

Who once was here but has now gone back;

Where back is, is not too clear,

But it's where Jack was before he was here;

So say farewell to Jack the Rover,

He's gone back to back and his journey's over.

Jack Ousbey

Last Laugh

R.I.P.

Here lies the body

of Hector Noakes,

who always laughed

at his own jokes.

His last laugh came

whilst epitaphing –

he split his sides

and so died laughing.

Liz Brownlee

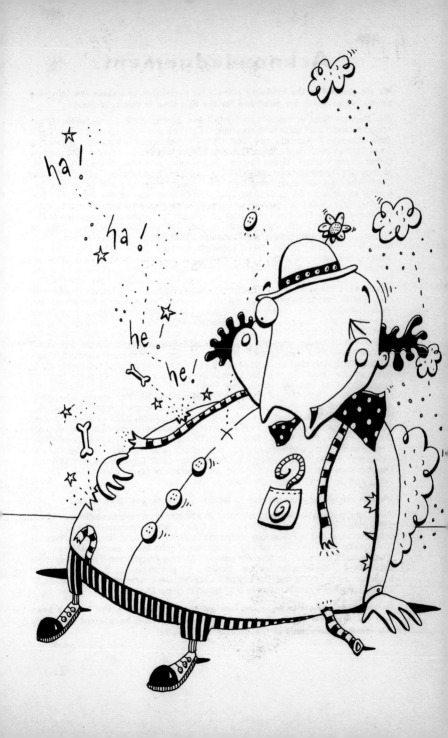

Acknowledgements

We are grateful to the following authors for permission to include the following poems, all of which are published for the first time in this collection:

Ann Bonner: 'Rest in Peace' copyright © Ann Bonner 2002; Liz Brownlee 'Grave Anagram' and 'Last Laugh' both copyright © Liz Brownlee 2002; Richard Caley 'Count Zoffin' copyright © Richard Caley 2002; Carol Carman 'Susan Steps Down' copyright © Carol Carman 2002; Jane Clarke: 'Ruth Lies Still' copyright © Jane Clarke 2002; Andrew Collett: 'Traffic Warden', 'Green Fingers', 'Dead Money' and 'Rosehip the Fortune Teller' all copyright © Andrew Collett 2002; Bill Condon: 'Larry the Liar' copyright © Bill Condon 2002; Paul Cookson: 'Judgement Day', 'Two Dinosaur Epitaphs' and 'Death of a Dog Burglar' all copyright © Paul Cookson 2002; Sue Cowling: 'Just As Well' copyright © Sue Cowling 2002; Gina Douthwaite: 'Epitaph to the Late Henry Hackett' copyright © Gina Douthwaite 2002; Eric Finney: 'Almost an Epitaph' and 'Here Lies' copyright © Eric Finney 2002; John Foster 'Percy Thistle: Football Referee', 'Miss Chit-Chat', 'Charlotte Cul-de-sac', 'Reginald Hacking' and 'Constable Chest' all copyright © John Foster 2002; Mary Green: 'Funny Bones Jones' copyright © Mary Green 2002; Trevor Harvey: 'Bridging the Cavity' copyright © Trevor Harvey 2002; John Kitching: 'Nursery Epitaphs', 'Grave Consequences' and 'Highway Endings' all copyright © John Kitching 2002; Daphne Kitching: 'Epitaph to a Victim of Designer Fashion' and 'Our Hamster Patches' copyright © Daphne Kitching 2002; Patricia Leighton: 'Epitaph to a Demon Headmaster' copyright © Patricia Leighton 2002; J. Patrick Lewis: 'Epitaph for a Know-it-all' and 'Passed Professionals' copyright © J. Patrick Lewis 2002; Wes Magee: 'Hiya,Cynth' copyright © Wes Magee 2002; Colin Macfarlane: 'A Sticky End' copyright © Colin Macfarlane 2002; Trevor Millum: 'Epitaph for Elijah' copyright © Trevor Millum 2002; Pat Moon: 'With Us Always' copyright © Pat Moon 2002; Frances Nagle: 'Cut Off' copyright © Frances Nagle 2002; Jack Ousbey: 'Resting Pets' and 'Back to Back' copyright © Jack Ousbey 2002; Andrew Peters: 'In Memory of Fido' copyright © Andrew Peters 2002; Cynthia Rider: 'Jane', 'Some Grave Consequences of School Trips to Castles' and 'The Escapologist' all copyright © Cynthia Rider 2002; Coral Rumble: 'In a Country Churchyard' copyright © Coral Rumble 2002; Andrea Shavick: 'The Teacher' copyright © Andrea Shavick 2002; Roger Stevens: 'My Thin Friend' copyright © Roger Stevens 2002; Marian Swinger: 'The Strong Man' copyright © Marian Swinger 2002; Charles Thomson: 'Speeding Vicar' copyright © Charles Thomson 2002; Kaye Umansky: 'Dracula' copyright © Kaye Umansky 2002; Ruth Underhill 'Dutch Courage' copyright © Ruth Underhill 2002; Celia Warren: 'R.I.P.' and 'Slipped Away' copyright © Celia Warren 2002; Clive Webster 'Epitaph for Frankenstein' copyright © Clive Webster 2002; David Whitehead: 'Unhappy Landing' copyright © David Whitehead 2002; Brenda Williams: 'Jamie Jack', 'Tommy Twigg' and 'Georgina' all copyright © Brenda Williams 2002.

We also acknowledge permission to include previously published poems:

John Cunliffe: 'On a Weaver' from Standing on a Strawberry (Andre Deutsch) copyright © 1987 John Cunliffe. Used by permission of David Higham Associates; Roy Fuller: 'A schoolmistress' and 'A Precocious Insomniac Tot' from The World Through the Window (Blackie) by Roy Fuller, included by permission of John Fuller; Lindsay Macrae: 'Jim "Houseproud" Groover' 'Annabel Smedley', 'Dithering Freddy' and 'Fast Away' both copyright © 1995 Lindsay Macrae, included by permission of the author; Roger McGough; 'Lady Godiva' and 'The Boy on the Burning Deck' copyright © Roger McGough 2002. Reprinted by permission of PFD on behalf of Roger McGough.

Despite every effort to trace and contact copyright holders, this has not been possible in a few cases. If notified, the publisher will be pleased to rectify any errors or omissions at the earliest opportunity.